3 4143 12003 5082

D0230061

SAY IT!

Charlotte Zolotow

illustrated by

Charlotte Voake

WALKER BOOKS
AND SUBSIDIARIES
LONDON • BOSTON • SYDNEY • AUCKLAND

For Hawa Diallo, Corinne Wells, Sharon Douglas, and Carlene Gabidon: four women who said it. And Charlotte heard. In her memory, with my love and gratitude, Crescent Dragonwagon ❖ To Oliver and Jen, Charlotte Voake

First published 1980 by Greenwillow Press • This edition published 2015 by Walker Books Ltd, 87 Vauxhall Walk, London SE11 5HJ • Text © 1980 Charlotte Zolotow Trust • Illustrations © 2015 Charlotte Voake • The right of Charlotte Zolotow and Charlotte Voake to be identified as author and illustrator respectively of this work has been asserted by them in accordance with the Copyright, Designs and Patents Act 1988 • This book has been typeset in Stemple Scheidner Roman • Printed in China • All rights reserved • No part of this book may be reproduced, transmitted or stored in an information retrieval system in any form or by any means, graphic, electronic or mechanical, including photocopying, taping and recording, without prior written permission from the publisher. British Library Cataloguing in Publication Data: a catalogue record for this book is available from the British Library • ISBN 978-1-4063-5211-5 • www.walker.co.uk • 10 9 8 7 6 5 4 3 2 1

It was a golden,
windy autumn day.

The leaves swirled round in the air
and on the ground as the little girl and
her mother walked down the road.

The little girl ran ahead,
kicking up the leaves,
and then came running back
and pulled at her mother's hand.

"Say it," she said.
"Come on, say *it!*"

"It's a wild, wondrous, dazzling day,"
   said her mother, laughing.

"No, not that,"
   said the little girl.

Just then, a small black kitten scampered
down a driveway and stood paw deep
in a pool of orange and brown leaves.

"What a black little cat you are,"
said the mother.

The little cat curved its paw and went
scrambling away in a scurry of leaves.
The mother and her little girl
went scuffing and scrunching
round a curve.

They came to a small pond.
The wind quietened down
and the trees in the water were still.
But as they watched, the wind began again,
and the trees in the pond shivered
into a million zigzagging
streaks of colour.

"Look," the little girl said.

"I am," said the mother.
"I'm looking."

The little girl tugged at her hand.
"Come on, say it," she said.

"It's magic," said her mother.
"It's a golden, shining,
  splendiferous day!"

"No," said the little girl.
"That's not what I mean."

They walked along swinging hands.
The clouds were grey-purple with the sun behind.
The little girl looked sideways at her mother,
waiting for her to speak.

A big dog came leaping out of the field
barking at them.

"Nice boy," said the little girl and he ran over
to be patted, wagging his big tail so it swept up
a spray of leaves from the ground.

"Say it," the little girl said,
looking straight at her mother
as their hands met in the dog's long fur.

"Nice dog, good dog," said the mother,
"fine boy, what amber eyes you have!"

"No," said the little girl.

A piece of fluff from some milkweed floated by.
The little girl caught the fluff in her fingers.

"Look!" she said to her mother.

"It's lovely," her mother said,
"a little floating cloud full of seeds."

They walked on past a brook
flowing down from the pond.
It bubbled over mossy green rocks and made
a muttering water sound that drowned
out the *crunch scrunch* of their steps.

A few steps more and they came to their own road
through the meadow and turned up the lane
leading to their house. Smoke was coming out
of the chimney, which
meant the little girl's father
had made a fire
to welcome them home.

Wild asters bent from side
to side in the wind. The leaves
blew in swirling circles over their heads.
It blew the little girl's hair straight up,
and the mother's as well, and made them both laugh.

The little girl ran up to her mother
and flung her arms around her.
The purple clouds blew into the chimney smoke,
the leaves swirled around them,
and the mother picked the little girl up.

"Say it," shrieked the little girl.
"Say it,
say it,
say it!"

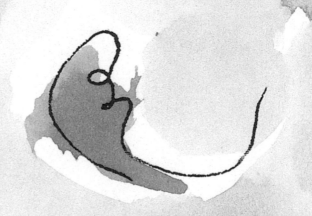

"I love you,"
said her mother.

"I love you,
I love you,
I love
you!"

And she twirled round and round
with the little girl in her arms until they
were both dizzy.

"That's what I wanted
you to say,"
said the little girl.

"That's what
I've been saying
all the time,"
her mother said,
laughing.

And she let the little girl slip gently
to the ground and took her hand as they
walked up the steps to their door.